Whoosh! There They Go!

A Slide-tacular Adventure

Written by The Salimarkles   Illustrated by Nathalie Kranich

For permission or ordering requests, please contact: info@salimarkle.com

Book design by the Virtual Paintbrush.

ISBN 978-1-7365056-0-1 (Hardcover)
ISBN 978-1-7365056-1-8 (Paperback)
ISBN 978-1-7365056-2-5 (Epub)
ISBN 978-1-7365056-3-2 (Kindle)

Library of Congress Control Number: 2021902328

Published in Encinitas, CA.

For Amaya and Zavier:
May your love for adventure, exploration, and discovery
lead you to a lifetime of wonder and happiness.

To our furbabies, Daji and Kundu,
thank you for always willingly accompanying us
on our adventures, both near & far.

Amaya and Zavi love to play,
exploring the world every day.
They find adventures wherever they are.
Their imaginations take them near and far!

Amaya shouts, **"Here we go!"**
Zavi yells, **"Let's go slow!"**

They travel the world searching for slides.
Watch them now as they **whoosh** by.

Up the hill and through the trees,
Hold on tight, here comes a breeze!

Now they're at the top.
Does this slide ever stop?

Whoosh!

There they go!

Amaya says, "This sand is hot!"
Zavi shouts, "This slide is hotter!"

Off in the distance what do they spot?

They race to the bottom shouting, "It's water!"

Whoosh!
There they go!

Splash, splosh, splish. It's time to go swimming with the fish.

Down the waterslide they go.
Look out below!

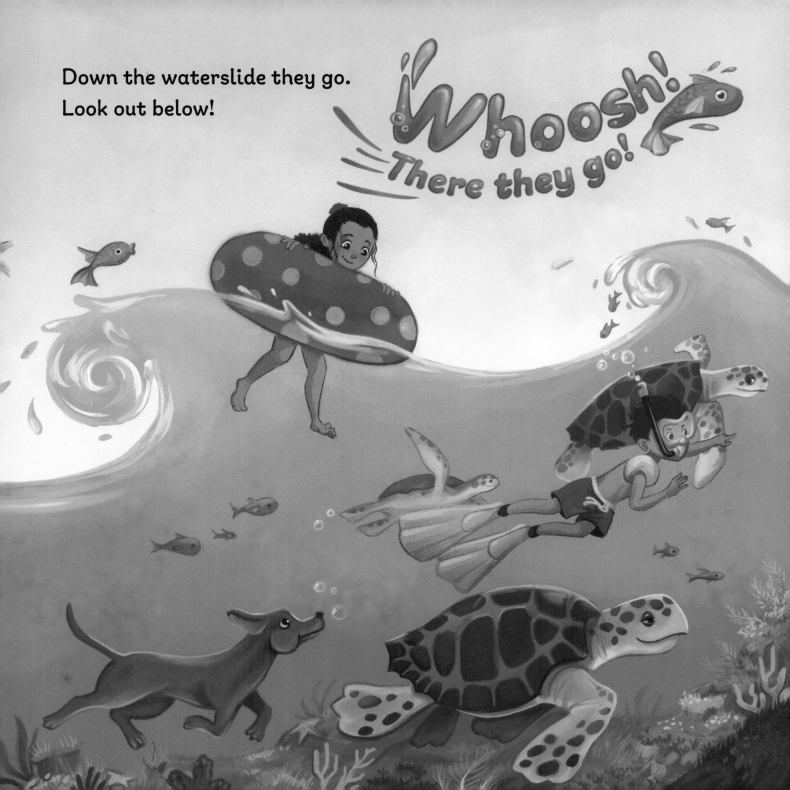

Brrrr, it's cold out here,
And the snow is getting deep.

The slide is nearly covered
So they take a running leap.

A dragon roars.
The children quake.
Amaya grabs its tail and gives it a shake.

Uh oh, time to...

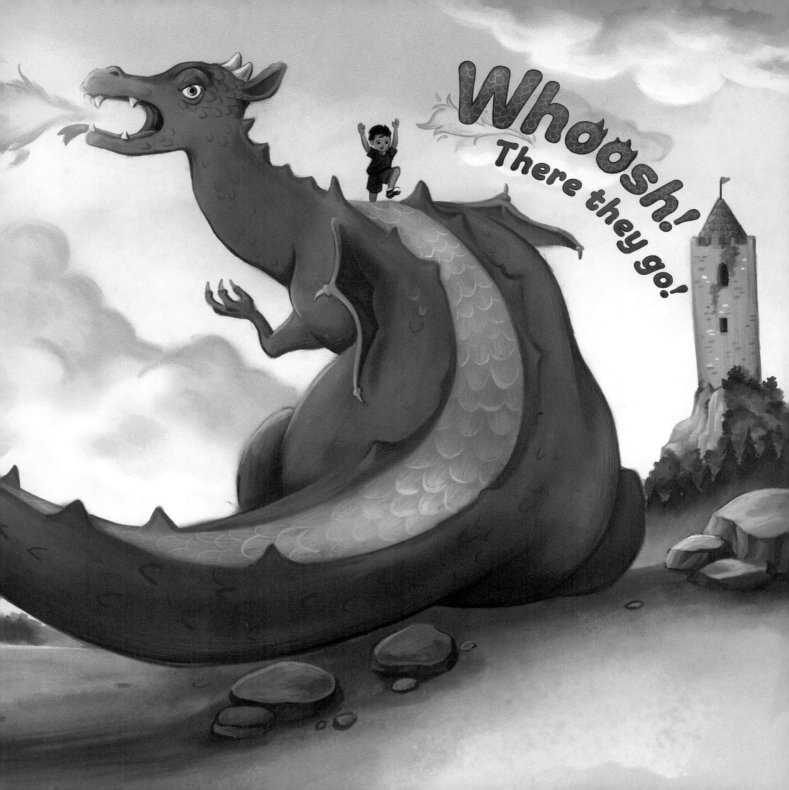

She sees a lion. He sees a bear.
The animals turn and give them a stare.
Let's race to the zoo down below.

It's getting late.
It's getting dark.
Time for one last slide
Through the park.

ABOUT THE AUTHORS

The Salimarkles are a travel-happy family who never pass up a good adventure. Their adventuring has allowed David, Kara, Amaya, Zavier, Daji, and Kundu to live in the U.S., Switzerland, and the Philippines. A Salimarkle foot &/or paw has explored every continent except one.

ABOUT THE ILLUSTRATOR

Nathalie Kranich is a German born children's book illustrator. To this day, she is inspired by the fairytales she grew up on. Nathalie has hiked over 50 mountains with her family, and envisioned stories on each of these journeys.

At age 16, she jumped on a train to England looking for adventure. This is where her love for illustration found direction. Now she lives in a village near the sea in the garden of England and is dedicated to bringing colourful stories to life.